OSCAR AND HOO

THEO was born in France in 1963.

Theo grew up in Paris and spent three months every summer on a French island, running barefoot over sand dunes and swimming in the sea.
He collected stamps, stones, and - like Oscar - dreams.

He worked as a scientist in Montreal but soon returned to France to work with people, instead of computers! Theo has worked in children's television in the UK, France, Germany and Spain for more than ten years. "I have got my head in the clouds, but my feet on the ground," he says. "I believe that becoming an adult is not about forgetting childhood, but understanding it."

MICHAEL DUDOK DE WIT was born in Holland in 1953.

After school Michael studied etching in Geneva and animation in the UK, where he made his first film, *The Interview*.

As well as illustrating books, he teaches animation, and has directed and animated many award-winning commercials for television and cinema.

Michael's other short animated films include *The Monk and the Fish*, which won numerous prizes and was nominated for an Oscar at the Academy Awards, and *Tom Sweep*. His latest film, *Father and Daughter*, won both an Oscar and a BAFTA award.

To all heads in clouds, especially Emil, Jane and Sophie, T.

To Alexander and Maya, M. D. d. W.

"It is the cinematic quality that makes this story of how Oscar is rescued by a cloud after losing his parents so impressive. With skilful use of scale and space, the story builds in frames, evoking a dream-like sense of heat, sand and isolation that's profound and evocative" Independent Magazine

First published in hardback in Great Britain by HarperCollins Publishers Ltd in 2002
First published in paperback by Collins Picture Books in 2003

1 3 5 7 9 10 8 6 4 2
ISBN: 0-00-710794-3

Collins Picture Books is an imprint of the Children's Division, part of HarperCollins Publishers Ltd.

Text copyright © Theo 2002
Illustrations copyright © Michael Dudok de Wit 2002

The HarperCollins website address is: www.fireandwater.com

Printed in Belgium

Oscar and Hoo

WRITTEN BY **THEO**

ILLUSTRATED BY **MICHAEL DUDOK DE WIT**

An imprint of HarperCollinsPublishers

Oscar sits at his bedroom window, dreaming.

He looks out at the clouds and the rain and the

thunder that have come between him and the sky.

He sighs and dreams of somewhere high,

up above the clouds and below the stars.

This is the best place for his dreams.

Where's the rucksack... and the sun cream,

the maps and the passports?"

Oscar yawns and stretches. It's the holidays:

chaos and confusion as usual.

Oscar and his parents are
going on a very long journey
and everything is such a rush.

Suddenly, he is...

...all alone!

"Mum! Dad!

Where are you? Help!" No one answers.

Tears roll down Oscar's cheeks as

he shouts again and again.

Are his parents behind that dune?   Or that one?

Oscar runs, but he's alone between the sand
and the burning sky and he's afraid.

Oscar shouts again, but
he hears neither an
echo nor a reply.

Just then, a voice whispers to him...

"Little boy,
why are you
raining?"

Oscar looks round – but there's no one there.
"Who said that? Help, I'm lost! The desert
is too big for a little boy like me!"
"And the sky is too big for a little cloud like me!" says the voice.

Oscar looks up and there, just above
him, he sees a single, lonely cloud.
"Who are you?" demands Oscar.
"I am Hoo, and I've lost
my flock," says the
little cloud.

"I'm Oscar and I've lost my parents!"
As Oscar replies, he feels some
drops of water falling on his head.
"Why are you raining, Hoo?" asks Oscar.
"Because I'm sad and lonely like you," says Hoo.

"What shall we do?" cries Oscar.

"I want to go home."

"Maybe I can help," says Hoo. "From up here, I can see everything. I can look for your parents. And I can give you shade, and tell you about my friends, the birds, and our long journeys over land and sea."

"And I'll tell you about my dreams," says Oscar, "and about my parents, who are always forgetting things..."

And so Oscar and Hoo set off.
They begin their search and they tell
each other everything.

As night falls, Oscar is scared of the dark,
so Hoo changes into funny
shapes to make him laugh.

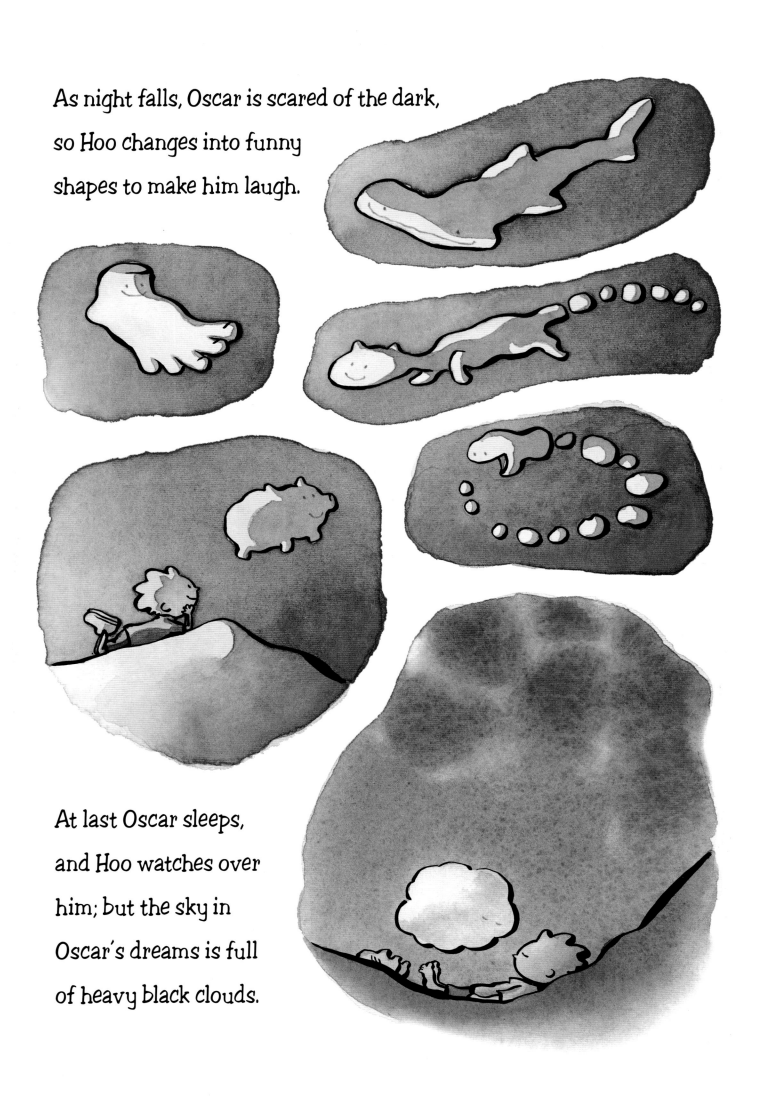

At last Oscar sleeps,
and Hoo watches over
him; but the sky in
Oscar's dreams is full
of heavy black clouds.

Next morning, when Oscar wakes, he's hungry and thirsty.

"Hoo, can you rain for me please, so I can drink?"

"But if I rain all my tears, I'll vanish," says Hoo sadly.

When he hears this Oscar starts crying. He thinks about his lost parents, and about poor Hoo who cannot cry.

Hoo comes closer and wraps himself around Oscar.

"Look, Oscar! Your tears have made me grow again," he shouts.

Oscar manages to smile but asks through his tears,

"Hoo, will I ever find my parents?"

So Hoo climbs up over the
dunes, higher and higher
into the sky, and looks
far into the distance.
Suddenly, he sees something
and, catching a breath of
wind, he flies nearer.
And yes, he's sure.

He shouts, "Oscar!
Quick! Over here!"
Oscar runs as fast as he
can, without stopping,
without looking back,
towards the something
that Hoo can see.

"Mum, Dad! Is it you?"

"Yes, yes, Oscar, we've found you at last!"

His parents rush towards him and they

all hug each other tight.

Hoo watches from above and

he can't help crying with happiness.

Back home, Oscar slowly recovers. His parents promise they will never lose him again.

Oscar returns to his window. He stares at the sky, dreaming...

...and he smiles.

"Hoo, promise you'll never leave me.
You're the best friend I've ever had!"
"Oscar, I give you my cloud's word; I'll never leave
you. You're the best friend *I've* ever had!"

Oscar and Hoo go everywhere together, but don't tell anyone.

It's their secret. And whenever Oscar is told that he's

got his head in the clouds, he laughs out loud. Wouldn't you?